INVISIBLE MESSAGE

Kitchen Experiment

By Meg Gaertner

Published by The Child's World®
1980 Lookout Drive • Mankato, MN 56003-1705
800-599-READ • www.childsworld.com

Photographs ©: Rick Orndorf, cover, 1, 14, 16, 17, 18, 19, 20, 21;
iStockphoto, 5, 13; Aleksandar Nakic/iStockphoto, 6; Mike Bi Ta/
Shutterstock Images, 8; Shutterstock Images, 9, 11, 12

ISBN 9781503825352
LCCN 2017959697

Printed in the United States of America
PA02378

Table of Contents

CHAPTER 1

Wet and Dry

Some things **absorb** water. A cotton sweater absorbs water from the washing machine. The fabric holds a lot of water. It takes a long time for the sweater to dry.

Some things **repel** water. A good raincoat repels water. The rain slips right off the raincoat. The water is not absorbed. A raincoat dries quickly.

Why do some things absorb water and others repel it? It has to do with their **molecules**. Molecules are made of different types of **atoms**. Everything is made of atoms.

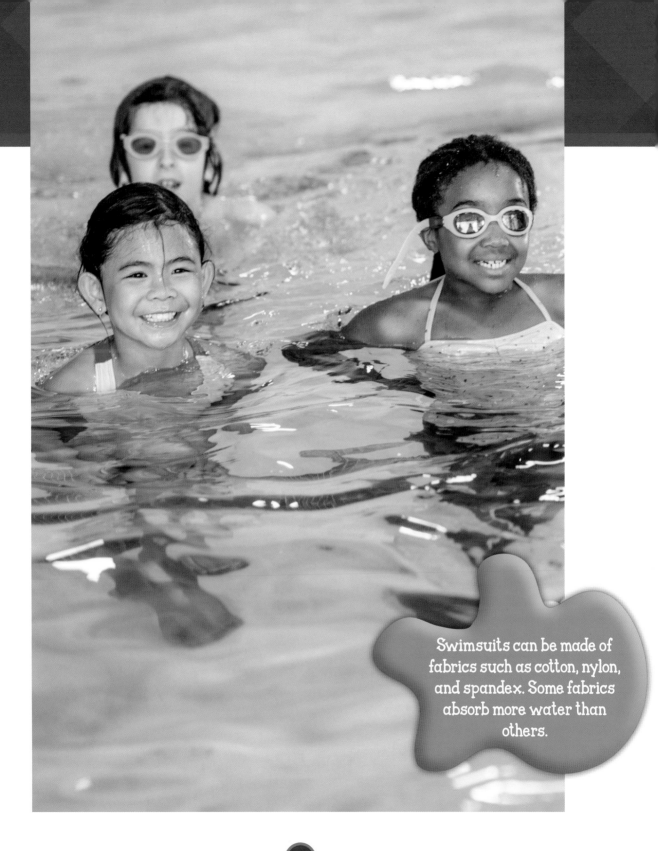

Swimsuits can be made of fabrics such as cotton, nylon, and spandex. Some fabrics absorb more water than others.

We can build models of atoms and molecules. This helps us understand their shapes.

6

Atoms are very tiny. We can't see them without special machines.

Some molecules mix well together. Sugar molecules mix well with water molecules. This means that sugar is **soluble** in water. The water molecules spread out. The sugar molecules come in between them. Then the water and sugar molecules stay together.

Other types of molecules do not mix well together. Oil molecules do not mix well with water molecules. This means that oil is **insoluble** in water.

TIP

Ducks use oil to keep their feathers dry when they swim. Their bodies make an oil. Ducks use their beaks to spread it over their feathers. Then their feathers do not absorb water. Water slides right off the duck.

Sugar mixes well with water. We stir sugar into drinks such as lemonade and iced tea.

If you put oil and water in a cup, they do not mix. The oil floats to the top of the cup. The water stays on the bottom of the cup. The oil repels the water.

These two liquids do not mix well together. We can see the layers.

CHAPTER 2

Hidden Wax Messages

Wax is a type of solid. It is insoluble in water. Wax molecules do not spread out in water. The wax repels the water. You can use wax to write an **invisible** message. No one will be able to see the message until you reveal it.

There are many different kinds of wax. Some kinds are made by animals. Bees make beeswax. They use it to build their hives. Some kinds of wax are made from plants. Soy wax is made from soybeans.

Honey is stored inside a honeycomb. The honeycomb is made of beeswax.

Some wax is man-made. Paraffin wax is used to make candles, crayons, and other things. Little bits of wax rub off a crayon when you draw. They can stick to the paper.

TIP
Beeswax and soy wax can also be used to make candles!

Crayons come in many different colors.

This is why crayons become smaller over time. A blue crayon leaves blue wax on paper. A white crayon leaves white wax on paper. White wax is hard to see on white paper. A message written in white crayon will be almost invisible on white paper.

Watercolor paints spread out on paper. The water makes the paper wet.

You can use watercolor paints to reveal your invisible message. Watercolor paints are mixed with water. When you paint over the hidden message, the paper absorbs the paint. The wax repels the paint. The message in white crayon can be seen through the paint.

CHAPTER 3

THE EXPERIMENT
Let's Write a Message!

TIME TO FINISH: 5-10 minutes

5
10

MATERIALS LIST

white crayon (not washable)
white paper
glass or cup
water
paintbrush
watercolor paint

TIP
Your message can also be a drawing.

1. Write your message on the paper with the white crayon. Press hard with the crayon. You want to leave lots of wax behind.

2. When you are ready to show your message, pour the water into the glass.

3. Dip the paintbrush in the glass of water.

4. Dip the paintbrush into one of the watercolor paints.

TIP

Any color paint will work. Dark colors such as blue and purple will work best. It will be easier to see your message.

5. Brush your paintbrush over the paper.

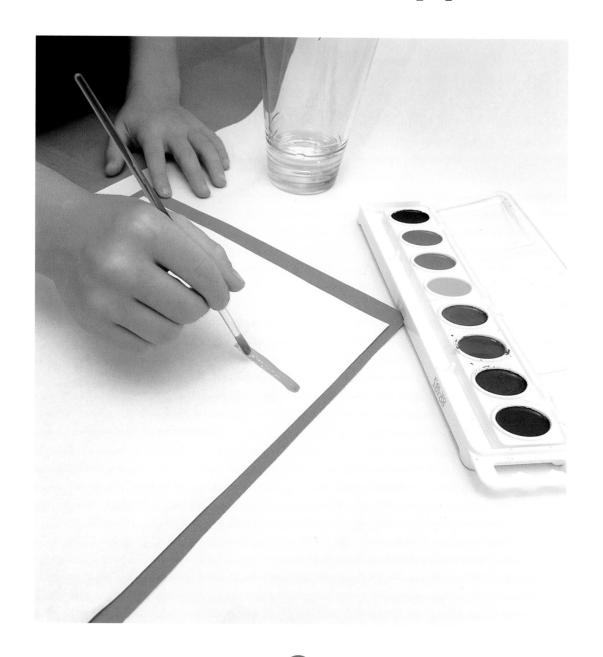

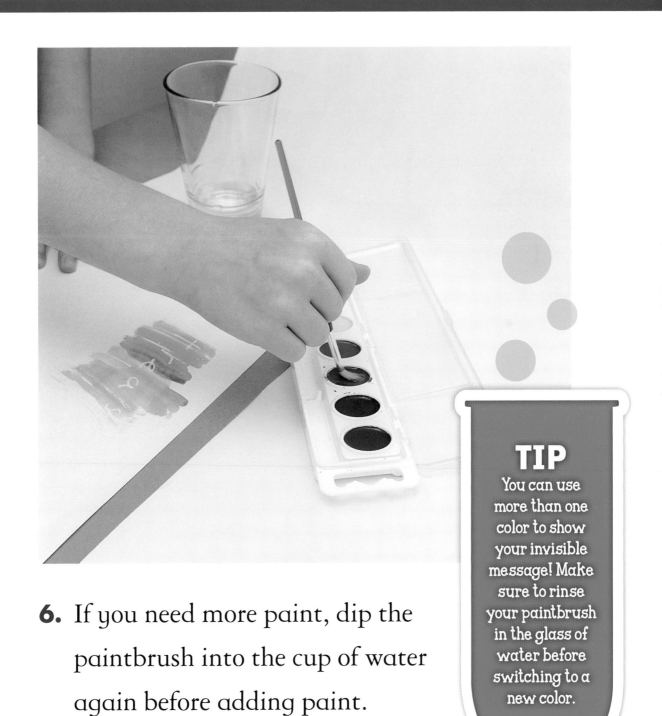

6. If you need more paint, dip the paintbrush into the cup of water again before adding paint.

7. Observe your hidden message. Can you see the whole message? How might you use invisible messages to talk to a friend?

Glossary

absorb (ab-ZORB) To absorb is to take something in. Paper absorbs water.

atoms (AT-uhms) Atoms are the tiny bits that make up everything. Atoms come together to make molecules.

insoluble (in-SOL-yuh-buhl) Something that is insoluble does not mix well with water. Wax is insoluble in water.

invisible (in-VIZ-uh-buhl) Something that is invisible cannot be seen. A message in white crayon on white paper is invisible.

molecules (MOL-uh-kyools) Molecules are groups of atoms. Sugar molecules mix well with water molecules.

repel (ri-PEL) To repel is to keep something away. Wax molecules repel water.

soluble (SOL-yuh-buhl) Something that is soluble mixes well with water. Sugar is soluble in water.

wax (WAX) Wax is a type of solid that repels water. Candles and crayons are made from wax.

To Learn More

In the Library

Akass, Susan. *My First Science Book*. New York, NY: CICO Books, 2015.

Higgins, Nadia. *Discover Water*. Mankato, MN: The Child's World, 2015.

Owen, Ruth. *Let's Investigate Everyday Materials*. New York, NY: Ruby Tuesday, 2017.

On the Web

Visit our Web site for links about invisible messages: **childsworld.com/links**

Note to Parents, Teachers, and Librarians: We routinely verify our Web links to make sure they are safe and active sites. So encourage your readers to check them out!

Index

About the Author

Meg Gaertner is a children's book author and editor who lives in Minnesota. When not writing, she enjoys dancing and spending time outdoors.